A DAY AT THE BEACH

a novel

by

William Freeman

cover art by Starr Emerson

Dedication

To Nona and Nono

Other works by the author:

A Gift for a Lifetime (short stories)
Murder in Key West (novel)
The Girl in the Black Boots (novel)
Money Bay (screenplay)
Ernest Hemingway's The Fifth Column (screen treatment)
Credit-Life (stageplay)

CHAPTER ONE

1.

When they were younger they never thought of defeat, disaster or death. Time would steal their innocence. They did not think the laughter would ever end or the sun would not shine. Life was like a day at the beach.

The Contessa's A frame house sat above the dunes overlooking an endless shoreline in both direction from its large wooden deck. They were in the middle of a crescent with neither end visible to the north or south. It was summer and most of the family would be there. And there were always a few friends who might come by for a day at the beach.

A path through the sea oats and brambles led up over the dunes and down to the beach. The sun had already risen above the horizon and was reflected in the waves. A family of dolphins swam just beyond the breakers.

Waterfall and Willie were two of the early morning walkers, barefoot in swim suits. They stopped from time to time to observe the life and relics at the water's edge. It was their world.

There were coquinas, small mollusks in the thousands that buried themselves in the sand as the water came in and left little bubbles when the water went back out revealing where they hid.

" We need to get a bucket, " Waterfall said. "you can rinse the sand out in a colander. Then make them into a broth. It taste like the sea, with a little butter and hot sauce."

There were mullet jumping in the slough between two sandbars. Schools of the fish moved as dark clouds beneath the surface. Willie swung an invisible net out toward the fish.

"Twenty with one toss," Willie bragged.

"I've heard that story before, " Waterfall said. "but what have you done for me lately?"

"That's a five, " Willie said exercising his fifth amendment right to silence.

"Are you still going to New York with Steve ?" she asked without looking up from her exploration of the broken shells and occasional sharks teeth that were a treasure.

"I wish I had my net," Willie said shading his eyes with his hands looking out at the schools and the sunrise.

"We're waiting for a call from Alfred Rice, Hemingway's lawyer."

Waterfall was lean without losing her shape in a one piece swimmers suit cut high at the hip. She had her goggles dangling from her wrist. She was tan everywhere you could see her skin and then some. Her hair was dark, streaked blonde by the sun down to her shoulders. As water came in around her feet, she turned and ran into the surf. When the water was above her knees she did a shallow dive into the face of an oncoming wave, swam under it and came out on the sandbar. She stood up in the waist high water after stooping down to wet her hair so that it flowed back away from her face as she surfaced to pull her goggles over her head. She turned her back to the beach and swam out to where the dolphins played.

2.

Willie was between money. That was the writer's way of life. And that's the show business. He needed to go to New York. He and Steve were producing Ernest Hemingway's only stage play THE FIFTH COLUMN on Broadway. That gave them the right to negotiate a movie which they also wanted to produce.

Willie loved New York. They had lived there for a year when Willie and Waterfall were producing a play he had written, CREDIT-LIFE, a trailer park melodrama in three acts. He had an education in the arts in college, professed by Harold Burris-Meyer who invented the smoke screen and camouflage during WWII, and had flown with the Laffeyette Escadrille in WWI. On the wall of his office was a Bill Mauldin cartoon of a G.I. asking an

officer standing in front of a bush, "
Okay professor, where'd you hide
my tank?"

The Professor had preached: "
Upstage foot ahead of the down-
stage foot." "Whisper to the last seat
in the house." and "never use your
own money."

"Other peoples money," Steve
had told him."Producing a play
gives us the right to sell shares,
partnerships and tee shirts."

It was hard to think about business when the waves showed such
perfect form and Waterfall was riding in the curl in front of him. He
was into the next wave and out the
back swimming toward the sand
bar where Waterfall was standing
up rinsing the sand out of her swim

suit. When he reached her they swam further out beyond the breakers and floated up and down in the swells. They tred water and looked at the horizon on top of a roller. Streaks of pink were re-flected on the water.

"Red sky at morning," Waterfall said.

"Sailor take warning," Willie fin-ished the thought. "Red sky at night, sailor's delight."

" I can remember some mornings on the boat with incredible blue skies, " Waterfall said. "and the days stayed perfectly beautiful."

"It's so pretty to think so," Willie said.

They were living on the boat, a forty one foot trimaran making un-

derwater videos when Waterfall
had to go back to the beach house
to take care of her mother, the
Contessa.

"I choose to remember only the
good days, " Waterfall said as they
both watched out to sea for the next
set.

They both started swimming at
the same time, but she had a slight
lead and caught the wave while it
washed under him. He listened to
her laugh in the curl and paddled a
little closer in. The second wave
was a double that would lose half
its force when it broke, but the third
wave was far out but already had a
small break at the top that spilled
down the face of the wave. He
could feel the water being pull out

into the vortex of the oncoming wave. He sank in the trough and started to swim fast hard strokes to get in front of the wave as it rose and to stay ahead of the break as it curled being pushed ahead of the rushing water. He turned as the wave caught him looked down the sun lit tube of the curl then was rolled over the falls and down into the sand. He was a little scraped but it was worth it.

" Who's coming today?" Willie asked.

3.

They were way out now beyond the sounds of the beach left only with the song of the sea. They floated on their backs and looked at the sky. The wind was coming out of the north. They looked at each other and began the long swim to shore riding the swell and the waves until they came to a depth where they could walk to the shore.

"Man'o war," Waterfall said and pointed to the blue bubble with the dark tentacles that stretched far back into the water. They stepped around the creature inspecting the blue sail like bubble that was its only power to be moved by the wind and tides trailing the lethal threads that burned like hell.

"We'll have to get a bottle of ammonia to carry with us," Willie said looking for a pocket in his brief suit. As his hands went over his belly, he could feel that he was firm and lean from the boat life.

It was her boat and she never let him forget it. She bought it. She also owned the big house down-town, but he owned the one next to it to be close to the kids. He had spent the last of his cash on that house and was living off of a settlement from a back injury in an accident last year. Waterfall had let him recover in a room in her house in exchange for him captaining her boat and getting it ready to do underwater videos. She was Cousteau inspired and quoted him often after she had interviewed him. He had one of her paintings and she had the interview.

"People protect what they love," she said.

When Willie was in the water he was buoyant. He carried no weight on his back and his limbs could move with the sea. He would take long deep breaths and thank God for his life. Then he would swim with the motion of a dolphin, his back arching and flexing as he dove down and turned upward.

"I taught you everything you know," Waterfall said. " I grew up in Coconut Grove. Pittsburgh is a long way from the beach."

"I didn't really learn to swim until I was in the Air Force," Willie said. "That and survival training are my carry over skills."

They walked up over the hard-pack to the soft sand and then the dunes. They stopped at the foot of the stairs the led up to the walkway across to the front deck of the A Frame. They were out of the wind between the dunes.

"Is Steve coming with the money?" Waterfall asked.

"The thirty million," Willie laughed.

" Do you think he's lying? " She asked.

"He's my Jewish Accountant, " Willie said. "How much is two and two ? How much do you want it to be"

They walked up the step to the walkway and turned back to watch the ocean. Waterfall pointed to the distant horizon. A large black ray jumped far enough out of the water that you could see the white of its belly.

"Captain Mark's wife called to say he might be late because he was arrested in Nigeria but the oil company that owns his boat got him out."

"He's been a bad boy again. I can't wait to hear this story, " Waterfall said. "He's always slightly innocent."

"The Contessa said that Captain Mark wont be allowed to smoke on the deck."

"Anything?"

"Anything."

"It's her house," Waterfall said. "She built it. It will always be her house."

"She said she was leaving it to you," Willie said.

"Don't you think my brother Cal will have something to say about it. He'll be here today with my Auntie and Uncle."

"Your mother always told me '" Willie said. "She lived far enough off of the interstate that her relatives from up north never had time enough to stop on the way back and forth to their condos down south."

"Sometimes they would call from the interstate to tell her they were passing by but didn't have time to stop," Waterfall said.

"So this visit today must be important," Willie said.

4.

The Contessa was sitting on the deck in her orange kaftan with a Dalmatian at each side and a great dane behind her. An old black dog with a white face lay at the foot of the chaise where she reclined. Her white hair was full and combed out. She wore bright red lipstick and large golden earrings. On one hand she wore a large pink jeweled ring that sparkled as she petted one of her dogs.

"Where is my coffee?" She yelled to Waterfall and Willie as they came up from the beach.

To one side of the deck where the ramp to the beach began, there was a shower stall where they rinsed the sand from their feet. Then Waterfall walked over to her mother and kissed her on the forehead. Willie walked past them and went inside.

"Yess'am," he said.

"I thought you were never going to get up,"Waterfall said to her mother. "We waited for you."

"I saw the interview you did with the Cousteaus," the Contessa changed the subject. "It was very good but there wasn't enough of you in it."

"Talk to Willie," Waterfall said. " He was the director. He ran the camera."

"I think he's jealous of you," the Contessa said. "You always get all of the attention. You always have. And he is living off of your money."

She turned away from her daughter and looked toward the house where Willie was coming out with a tray of demitasse cups, coffee, cream and sugar. There was a small iron table to one side where a dog wasn't and he set it all down and poured three cups.

"Get a few dollars out of my purse," the Contessa said. "Go down to the beach and buy some fish from the fishermen. Be sure you get enough."

"Go, go," Waterfall laughed. "What are you waiting for?"

"Yess'am," Willie said and drained one of the cups. He picked up a pair of binoculars that were kept on the deck near the shower and scanned the crescent until he saw them about a mile to the south. He pulled up his trunks and was off on a mission.

The fishermen used two pickup trucks. One truck hauled a dory with the net on a trailer. Six men from both trucks launched the boat as the truck backed it into the water. The truck then unhooked the trailer and rolled it out of the way while two men in the boat began to offload one end of the net which was tied to hitch on the back of the truck.

The boat started up and headed into the waves out past the breakers setting the net in a large arc until it beached itself fifty yards from where it started. The other end of the net was secured to a hitch on the second truck and they began to haul in the catch.

The trucks backed down to the waterline, picked up a section of the net and pulled it up onto the beach, backed down again picked up more net and hauled it up until fish could be seen jumping as the net came into the shallows. Then all the men waded out and finished pulling in the net by hand until the catch was up out of the water and they began to cull, tossing out trash fish and throwing the valuable fish into a large tub in the back of one of the trucks.

" I want to buy some fish," Willie told a sunburnt man in a red ball cap who seemed to be in charge of the selection.

"Keep the shark," he yelled to his crew who picked up the three foot hammerhead by the tail and threw him up onto the sand still thrashing reaching exhaustion.

Waterfall made another pot of espresso for her mother and brought it out onto the deck. The Contessa was breathing deeply with her eyes closed. She felt the sun on her tan face. She was still beautiful after all these years. She wore big earrings so no one would notice the wrinkles.

"I want you to always keep it open to our family. The kids like to come down each summer for a couple of weeks," the Contessa told her.

"That's when I'll go on my vacation," Waterfall said.

"I'm not going to give you any money, just the house and the others can split up real estate, my mortgages, and cash."

"Mother, do what you want," Waterfall said. "You're a wealthy woman and you earned every penny of it including social security. Is there anything you need that you cant have. After all, you have your Mercedes."

They both laughed so hard it rattled the cups on the tray. They paused and sipped and felt the breeze. A line of pelicans flew in a line over them.

"So, what's he up to this time,?" the Contessa asked.

"He and Steve are producing a Broadway play," she said and took a towel from the shower and spread it on the deck to lay down. She stretched out and arched her back,

"You should have been a model," the Contessa said.

"I was a model, remember," Waterfall said.

"That's right, when you were in Italy," the Contessa laughed. "Sometimes I forget. "

"Why don't Auntie and Uncle like Willie?"

"Oh, they like him," the Contessa said. "It's just that they think he's living off of you."

"Because he's a writer and doesn't have a job. That his only real job is being your servant, making you coffee taking you to your treatments. Fixing your outside light."

"He fixes things," the Contessa waved it away. "That light hasn't worked right since he fixed it."

"You have to turn it on from inside the house. You have to keep it off at night so it doesn't confuse the nesting turtles. You only turn it on when you need it. Sometimes people come up from the beach at night and break into empty beach houses."

"I have my dogs ," the Contessa pet the two closest to her. "Willie does help me out, but where was my coffee this morning?"

"He is your servant, " Waterfall teased her.

"I"m lucky to have a job, " Willie said.

He had come up out of the sunrise while they were looking away. There was the three foot shark in his hand held up in triumph. It was dead and gutted. The head was still on, its T shaped snout with an eye at each end. It had an open curved mouth lined with teeth. The body was grey and looked smooth.

"For an extra dollar, the fisherman cleaned him and got to keep the liver," Willie said.

He put the shark at the foot of the Contessa's chair and the dogs all crowded around to sniff.

"Get away," Willie yelled and picked the fish back up.

"Don't yell at my dogs," the Contessa said. "I'm the only one who can yell at them."

She reached over and touched the skin of the shark.

"It's like fine sand paper," she told Waterfall.

"And a face only a mother could love," Waterfall said. "With a mouth big enough to take your ring off your finger and the hand too."

The Contessa pulled her hand away and looked at the large pink sapphire. "Jack got this in a deal. It once belonged to Eva Peron. It was a pair of earring that I had made into two rings. I want you to have one."

"Do you have any milk," Willie said. "Enough to soak the meat.

They urinate through their skin,
The milk purifies the meat."

"Thanks for the advice," Waterfall made a face.

"Make enough for everybody," the Contessa said after him as he went to work. "You never know who's going to show on a day like this."

Waterfall followed him inside. She had something to tell him. She gave him a sign.

The Contessa reclined on a chaise taking in her view.
She had cup of coffee in one hand and the other rubbed the big dog. At one time she would have had a cigarette too. It was fashionable at

the time. Everybody at the Bridge Club smoked. There were ashtrays on the dinner table. But, not in her Father's house when she was a girl.

"En'tabale," her mother would call and all eight children would come to the table with their father at the head. There should have been nine children but Hugo had an accident and died. He had bumped his head while riding a horse. Father thought he was all right and put him to bed with a headache. He died a few days later in that bed.

The Contessa was the youngest girl and Hugo had been the youngest boy and therefore they were close and both received a lot of Father's attention. He would look at all of them seated at the dinner table put out his hands and say "These are my precious jewels."

He was a Banker in Boston when his good friend Giannini started the Bank of America.

He had owned a Patent Leather factory in Palermo and was "black handed" by the Mafia. He turned the business over to them and came to America with money in his pocket.

People from the old country would send money back and forth and he banked it for them and his wife transcribed their correspondence since they couldn't read or write.

The Contessa could remember women making her mother write it over again if it wasn't read back with the same passion of the writer even though the words remained the same. It was only yesterday when she was a girl. Before she became a woman of substance and means. Before she knew that she was going to die.

"Are you going to get our eyes done again?" Waterfall came out with a brochure and a big pitcher of water.

"Throw it away," the Contessa said. "It's nothing. So what's happening with your career in the movies with the two big shots. His partner is coming over today? What for?"

"They're waiting for a phone call from New York," Waterfall said.

"They're waiting to hear that Mary Hemingway has signed the contract."

"How many years has he been waiting for that phone call?" the Contessa asked. " How many years have you two been together?"

"That's a five," Waterfall said. "That's a five."

They both took a deep breath and took in the view. The sky was now a brighter blue and cloudless. The sun had brightened beyond vision even with dark glasses. The air was warm as it moved across their skin. The breeze was out of the southeast. The ocean was dark green and a straight line at the horizon. White lines of cresting waves rolled over the sand bars and washed ashore. Occasionally a large wave would crash and you could hear its roar in the distance.

"I wish it would never end," the Contessa said.

5.

They watched their black cat
watching the mockingbird. When
the Contessa would return to the
beach house after being away for a
while, the black cat would bring her
a present: a dead rabbit, a large
dead rat and birds of various sizes
and origins. The small upper deck
that came out of the upstairs landing was strewn with dried bones of

different sizes and species. The black cat leaped from the lower deck to the upper deck railing with the ease of a ballerina. Above them a line of pelicans dipped their wings and rode the air current directly over them. A line of white pelican poop trailed across the deck and onto Waterfall.

"Money's coming," the Contessa said.

Waterfall stood up and looked at herself and laughed. She ran into the outside shower and cleaned herself. Even the cold water was warm.

Sea Oats and tall grasses waved in the dunes. Out on the horizon was the small white triangle of an offshore sailor. The sky had but one small white cloud.

"Isn't this the most beautiful place on earth," the Contessa said.

"Is Jack coming up today?" Willie asked when he joined them. He had some Italian goblets and a pitcher of ice water. All had glazed artwork and bright colors. The pitcher was shaped like a chicken with its beak turned upward as a spout.

"I don't know and I don't care," the Contessa said. "He'd rather stay down there in his office working on that appeal than come up here. He can go to hell!"

"He's been through a lot, mother," Waterfall said .

"He's been through a lot of money at the track," the Contessa was indignant.

"He went through that war, and they sent him to prison, " Waterfall said.

"You always stick up for him," the Contessa said. "You always take his side. He's your father, but one day you'll find out that some men just aren't worth it."

"Some men are," Waterfall winked at Willie.

The Contessa didn't say anything. She looked out at her view of the beach and petted one of the dogs. It was the old white faced black mongrel that the kids had picked up years ago when they found some redneck beating her.

They brought her home and kept her. She loved to have her throat stroked just like that. Her pink tongue hung out and she panted, then she turned a half circle and lay down on the deck in the shade from the large table set to one side where the three of them sat and talked.

"What about your father?," Willie asked the Contessa.

"He was a wonderful man," the Contessa said and closed her eyes and bowed her head. A hand across her forehead swept in memories. Poor Hugo. She had seen her father cry.

A young girl in a two piece bathing suit came out onto the deck. She was tan and her brown hair was sun bleached in places. She hugged Waterfall and kissed her. She was almost as tall as her mother and just as beautiful. She bent down and kissed the Contessa.

"You're up late," Willie said.

"I was up late reading your book," Sophia told her father. "I'm afraid to tell my friends. All That sex."

"That's not sex, it's erotica," Willie said. "It's an art form. Would you rather I write about violence and mayhem? Maybe wrestling, two ugly guys hugging each other. It just doesn't interest me."

"Has anyone else like my sister Rita read it?" she asked.

"No," Willie said ." Just you and your mother."

"When do I get to read it ?" the Contessa said.

"What did you think, Mom ?" she asked Waterfall.

"I liked it," Waterfall said. "Didn't you just hate the girl in it?"

"Exactly," she said. "But I really liked the cop."

" I read that one," the Contessa said. "You have to change the part about being in the war. You were never in a war."

"It's fiction," Willie said. " It's not about me. We also serve who only stand and wait. It's in the bible. I'll change it . It has nothing to do with the story. Editorial board meeting over."

A pretty girl with long blonde hair in her face wearing a red one piece bathing suit with a red cross came up from the beach. Her neck and shoulders were covered with red streaks. She came over and kissed the Contessa.

"Here's your big sister now,"Willie said.

"My goodness," the Contessa said looking at the streaks. "What happened to you?"

"This kid swam into a man of war and I had to go get him, Rita said. "It got me too, but we put some ammonia on it so it really doesn't hurt. They said if I didn't feel good I could take the rest of the day off. So, I told them I didn't feel good."

"You better go lay down," the Contessa said.

"I'm okey," Rita said. "Theres a party down the road that I wanted to go to anyway. Sophia you can go too."

They gave their parents and the Contessa a kiss goodbye and were gone.

The dogs suddenly stood up and started toward the stairway that came up from the driveway at the back of the house. Waterfall went to see who was coming. The dogs didn't bother to bark. It was no stranger.

6.

"Where's the money?" Waterfall said to Steve as he came dancing up the steps onto the deck. He gave her a big hug and a kiss. He patted her on the rear end.

In his own words, Steve was a "juicy morsel."

He was a little over five and a half feet tall with dark curly hair and a deep tan. He had strong handsome features sparkling dark eyes and a definite nose and sculpted chin. His body was lean with the definition of the artist's model he had been a few years ago. He never had any trouble getting girls. Girls came to him.

Steve stepped over a dog and leaned down to kiss the Contessa. The Contessa turned away and brushed him off. Steve feigned rejection.

"Don't you love me anymore?" Steve said.

"She thinks no partner is good enough for me," Willie said.

"And no woman," Waterfall said and they all laughed.

"Come here," the Contessa said and pulled Steve toward her. She pulled his head down and kissed him on the forehead.

"I hope that wasn't boche d'morta," Steve said.

"That's what they gave my father before he left Palermo," the Contessa said. "The kiss of death."

Steve stood up and looked out at the view from the deck. He took a deep breath and did the salutation to the sun. He brought his hands together above his head and bowed.

"If you kill me," Steve said. "Bury me here. Better yet, throw my ashes into the sea."

"Did you get the money?" Waterfall whispered in his ear.

"Thirty million," Steve said. "It's in a bank in the Cayman Islands."

"Let me go inside and put on my bathing suit," the Contessa said.

"You don't have to go inside," Steve said.

The Contessa brushed him off and went inside.

The three on the deck huddled together while the dogs moved into the shade.

"How did you do it?" Waterfall said.

" I'll tell you later," Steve said.

"Thirty million?" Willie said.

"In an account named Ernest Hemingway's The Fifth Column. In the Credit Suisse Investment Bank." Steve stated. "We're Fully Funded."

"We don't have to take money from anybody," Willie said.

"But we will," Steve said. "Did Alfred Rice call yet?"

"I told him we'd be at this number," Willie said.

The Contessa came back out in a flowered one piece suit and a big straw hat.

"I'm going for a dip," she said and picked up a towel from the shower.

"I'll go with you," Steve said and was out of his shirt and shorts with a brief speedo that showed off his strong legs. He had been a runner for years and finished in the top one hundred in the New York City Marathon. He took the Contessa's arm as they sashayed down to the beach. He always had a dirty joke to tell her and he made her laugh like a young girl, a young girl with a cough.

7.

The sun had risen higher as did the temperature. The upper deck now shaded the lower deck. The A Frame was all glass in the front with windows to the peak and sliding glass doors at every level. The beams that secured the glass formed a tall cross with a wooden chimney to one side that at one time rose as high as the top of the A but had been blown off in a hurricane and now was cut flush with the slanted roof.

The Contessa was inside with a towel wrapped around her waist making a pot of pasta. From the kitchen she could look out at the deck and the ocean and sky beyond. The kitchen was separated from a dining area by a counter with bar stools. The dining room table was round made of mahogany with a set of four large swivel chairs that could always be turned toward the view.

To the side was a large area with couches and tables and a television set in the fire place. Various pieces of stain glass work hung in the windows. At the back of the living room was a small hallway, two small bedrooms and a full bath. There was a stairway set against the wall that separated the hallway. It led up to the master bedroom on the next level where the Contessa had set up a desk and office and had built a bridge to the upper deck. In the ceiling above the office was a large square housing an exhaust fan that was blowing hot air out of a vent in the crawlspace beneath the roof.

The house had been built on pilings so it sat above the dunes leaving room for a garage and a rental unit down below that Jack had built. A circular drive at the back of the house leading to the street had been paved, as well as a carport under the deck that faced the sea. A wooden staircase led up top to the deck where they sat.

"Willie," the Contessa yelled. "Fix me a drink. Turn on a light. Thats's what my father used to say. He'd turn on a light and say 'the lights have been turned on' and pour himself a glass of wine."

Willie went inside leaving Waterfall and Steve on the deck in a lounge and a hammock that was strung between the supports of the upper deck.

" She built the first condominium in Miami," Waterfall told Steve. " She and my father owned over sixty houses and a small hotel on Miami Beach. We lived in Kodak's house on LaGorce Drive. He traded that for our house on Colony Road with the swimming pool and tennis court. But I was born and raised in Coconut Grove."

"Coconut Grove !" Steve said. "You think you're better than me.

I'm a New York Jew from the Bronx.
I once finished in the top one hundred in the New York City Marathon. You think you're better than
me?'

"Yes," Waterfall said. "Way better."

The Contessa came outside. She
unwrapped the towel around her
waist and still had her bathing suit
on. Willie came out behind her
holding two tall chilled glasses.

"Where's my drink," the Contessa said. Willie handed her one
glass and gave the other to Waterfall. Steve was nursing a beer. Willie had a glass full of water.

"I wanted to have 'the down below' ready for Captain Mark," the
Contessa said. "Because you never

know what will happen with him around."

"What's a captain Mark?" Steve said.

"He's our hero," Waterfall said. "He saved mother's life."

"You saved your mother's life," Willie said.

"What happened ?" Steve asked.

"It was nothing," the Contessa waved it away. "We were on my boat. It's a sixteen foot boat with a motor on the back. The top was down because Captain Mark was splitting the waves on our way out the inlet. It was too hot and I had a beer. I was stupid."

"I thought you could make it," Waterfall said. "You always were a good swimmer. "

"I ran out of breath," the Contessa said.

The Contessa closed her eyes for a few minutes. Steve was going to say something but Willie gave him a sign to be still. Waterfall put her arm around her mother's shoulder.

"I was scared to death," the Contessa said.

She thought about Hugo and her father. Her mother. Her first husband. The war. The Funerals. She was driving an ambulance when she met Jack. Life has a way of writing its own story, no matter how hard you try to make dreams come true.

8.

She was one of nine children in a large house outside Boston. Papa wanted to know where each of them was at all times. When one of the older girls was missing, her mother would always alibi that she was at the library.

"My geniuses, " Papa said. "They're always at the library studying."

Her father was an Italian Banker. She had been raised between Boston and Palermo where the family owned a large Villa. General Patton had made it his headquarters during the war. Her older sister still lived there having bought out all the siblings but for Franco who was still holding out so she couldn't sell the place.

" A surfboard," the Contessa said. "That is what got me the most beautiful place in the world."

They always lived in nice places when she and Jack were doing business in Miami, before he went to jail. Then she and Waterfall were left with nothing after the lawyers collected and the business stopped.

Waterfall had a boyfriend who was a surfer. They left Miami and went to Daytona Beach where they opened the first surf shop on the East Coast. They started building boards and renting and selling. Since surfers in general didn't work when the waves were good, they never had a lot of money so the Contessa sold boards on time with monthly payments. With Waterfall as the model and the first East Coast Women's Surfing Champion, they attracted quite a crowd.

When one boy had fallen seriously behind in his payments, the Contessa called his mother. The woman said she didn't have any money but she was making payments on a lot up the coast that they were never going to use. She was willing to trade her equity in the lot for the balance owed on her son's surfboard, if the Contessa was willing to take over the payments on the two thousand dollars she still owed. The lot was oceanfront and lots were selling for fifty dollars down, fifty a month all the way up and down the coast. She made the deal even though she and Waterfall were living day to day on the money from the surf shop.

"We used to drive up, " Wille said.

"He was our chauffeur," Waterfall said.

" I was lucky to have a job," Willie said. "We'd go to the court house to find the lot on a plat and then we'd drive around with a bad map trying to find it in the dunes. None of the roads were paved and there were more empty lots than houses. There was a big Blue Building on the beach. We were told that it was the Negro hotel and this was the black beach where the local colored people came on the weekends and holidays

" We would always find her lot because once we saw the blue hotel, there was a low block house two lots down from hers. We later learned that the pock marks in the blocks were from the time Martin Luther King had stayed there and was shot at. The Contessa's lot like most of the rest were covered with grasses, brambles, briars, brush and an occassional palm and lots of palmetto bushes. When we were there the first time , we wore sandals to get to the top of the dunes. We learned that we needed something sturdier against the thorns sand spurs and stinging nettles that protected the dune we climbed to get a view of the wide grey and white strip of hard packed sand big enough to land a jet on."

She never told Jack about the lot until after she had built her house on it. He would have traded it for something and then traded again and finally lost it gambling. That's what had happened in Miami.

She and Jack had fallen in love in Boston and got married much to the concern of her family. They had to get away. They flipped a coin, California or Florida.

It was just after the war. He was going to law school at the University of Miami and they were running a real estate business on the side. When his college buddies found out about her Italian heritage they all called her "The Contessa." The name suited her. The name stuck.

She was a war widow with a child. Her first husband had told the generals what to do. He was a meteorologist. He was the weatherman who told them which way the wind blows. He had recorded the strongest winds in the world on top of Mount Washington. He was killed in an accident on a mountain road. All of the flower shops in Boston were sold out for his funeral. They had a child together.

Jack was so handsome in his Captain's uniform. He was a friend of her girlfriends boyfriend who was a doctor at the hospital where they drove the ambulances for the boys who had come home but were not whole. He was a farm boy from Indiana who was a pilot in the Army. He never talked about the war.

Steve came outside with a bottle of champaign he had retrieved from his car. He had a bag full of plastic flutes. Waterfall and the Contessa sat at the table now shaded by the house as the sun moved farther west.

"Is this a celebration?" Willie asked. "Did Alfred call?"

"Not yet. I didn't want it to get warm," Steve said. "This is a toast too our gracious, gorgeous hostess."

He handed the first glass to the Contessa who accepted it graciously.

"Turn on the lights," the Contessa said ."That's what my father said in the afternoon when he had a drink, because in those days, no one drank before dark. Salute !"

" L'Chiam," Steve said. "And are you doing anything later tonight?"

"Go away," she said. "I hear you have a string of girls a mile long. What are we supposed to be celebrating?"

"Fully funded, " Steve said. "Ernest Hemingway's The Fifth

Column is fully funded. "I'll show you letter from the Bank. It's our letter of credit that we have money in the Bank."

"I don't have my glasses," the Contessa said. "But it looks very official. I can read the Credit Suisse in Gold."

He showed the letter to Willie who passed it on to Waterfall as Steve filled their glasses.

"Thirty million!" Waterfall read.

"You're all full of shit," the Contessa was upset." You sound just like Jack with all his wild ideas. You know what that got him."

"Well, I guess it got you here," Steve embraced the view.

"I got this place on my own," the Contessa said. "After Jack went to jail, we had nothing. The lawyers took it all. Waterfall and I were run out of town. I couldn't show my face at the bridge club anymore. She was hanging out with surfers and you know what they're like."

"I know," Waterfall said. "Don't rub it in."

"We opened that surf shop together," the Contessa said. " And I got this property as part payment on a surf board. And I built the house with the money I made on the mobile home park we developed down south."

"When Jack won his appeal and got out of jail," Waterfall said. "He opened a surf shop across the parking lot from us and rented boards. He lived in the back of the shop."

"He'd make enough money during the day so he could go to the track at night," the Contessa said.

"He had put a piece of property in his brother's name so he would have something when he got out," Waterfall said. "It's the property we developed that enables us to live in the grand style we do today."

"Jack loved it," the Contessa said. "He got to ride around on a big tractor just like he was back on the farm in Indiana."

"I was the well drilling man," Willie said. "I put in wells on all those lots."

"You are a man of hidden skills," Steve admired.

"He can also fix a deisel engine," Waterfall said.

"That's a different story, " Willie said. "I might write about it some day, so I can't talk about it. It's far too painful."

He showed Steve the back of his hand. One of the fingers was bent at an uncommon angle. Waterfall grabbed Willie's hand.

"Mon hero," she said.

"You never told me about that property," Steve said. "You've been holding out on me."

"I"ll tell you about it some other time," Willie said. "It's need to know."

"I'm your partner," Steve said. "I need to know."

"It's all Waterfall's," Willie said. "Enough said ?"

"Contessa ," Steve turned to his audience but directly to her. " Did I tell you about these two old Jews in Miami Beach? So one says, 'Sol, so how did you come here to retire?' Sol says, 'I had a clothing store. There was a fire. I lost every thing. I had insurance. How about you?'
The other guy says, 'I had a hardware store. There was a flood. We lost everything but I had insurance.'

Sol says, 'So how do you start a flood?' "

The Contessa laughed and went inside to check on the stove. Waterfall and Willie stayed on the deck with Steve.
The dogs were up again running to the top of the stairs and barking.

"I hope it's Captain Mark," Willie said. He usually brings something from his last trip."

"I've got a crate in the garage that he had shipped here when he got out of the Navy." the Contessa said. "It's been there a long time."

"Hello, Hello," a man could be heard above the dogs.

Then a woman called, "Darling, we're here."

The Contessa looked at Steve and rolled her eyes. She got up and went to the stairs and quieted the dogs. The day was getting hotter.

9.

The tide was coming in with a light wind from offshore. Swells had risen a couple of feet and curled over the sandbars. Surfers going out rode their boards on their bellies as they paddled out. They rode down the back of the first set of breakers and up under the rush of the next wave until they joined their buddies sitting on their boards bobbing as pelicans in staggered formation out beyond the waves.

They looked out to sea for the next set that would bring a perfect tube ride and a cutback and stand straight up all the way to the beach. Then turn around, go back out and do it all over again. In the distance three swells formed in succession.

A few of the surfers took that first wave that had such great form and dropped in and it dumped quickly sending them over the falls

"They say the third wave," Willie told Steve, "but in my experience the second is the best. You let it pass and then watch as it rolls into a tunnel of swirling light; blue , green, white and sometimes a rainbow at the end of the tube. And then that third wave sneaks up your back and you hold on and wait for the next set."

"Don't listen to him," Waterfall said. "He doesn't know what he's talking about. He's from Pittsburgh."

"And you, Champ, are from Coconut Grove,"Willie
said.

"Coconut Grove," Steve said. "You're not only beautiful but well bred. I"m impressed. You're so much more than a decoration."

"Just look at that water," Waterfall said. She looked back over her shoulder where her mother , her Auntie and her Uncle were exchanging hugs inside. Her brother

Cal was with them but hadn't announced himself delightfully surprising the Contessa.

"I need to take a dip."

"Who are these people?" Steve asked Willie as Waterfall went down to the beach.

Inside Auntie was looking over the Contessa's outfit, straightening it here and there. The Uncle hugged the Contessa and cast a sideways glance at the group out on the deck. Cal hugged his mother and rubbed her back.

"The wicked witch of the North," Willie said. "then there is Uncle, I'm not sure which one. And Waterfall's brother Cal, the saint."

"I didn't know she had a brother," Steve said.

"Don't get her started," Willie said. "She used to idolize him while they were growing up, but now there is no love lost."

To one side of the deck, seats had been built into the railing with a wooden table in front where they caught the morning sun for breakfast, and it was shaded in the afternoon by the house for lunch and sometimes dinner. In the winter, northeast winds drove them inside or to the house's leeward southern exposure.

The Contessa loved the way her animals and Waterfall would welcome her back. Waterfall took care of everything while she was away. She fed the animals and brought in things from the deck when a storm approached. The Contessa knew that Waterfall loved the beach house as much as she did. They had built it together while renting a small house on the other side of the highway. Willie was in California producing a play, The Last Comeback, that Waterfall had written.

The two women walked together thousands of times on the beach in all kinds of weather even when the dogs were smart enough to stay home. In the winter, they would walk with their capes wrapped around them against the wind. They would be the only ones on their beach.

"I'm going to give this place to you," the Contessa told Waterfall.

CHAPTER TWO

10.

"We were walking with the dogs on the beach," Waterfall said. "She said she wanted me to have the beach house. And I said I would keep it open to the family as she has in the past. Relatives from up north come through but never stay long. They got bored."

"What brought it on?" Willie asked her.

They were seated out at the end of the walkway overlooking the beach. The Contessa and family were inside. The dogs were in the shade.

"She was talking about when she was going to die," Waterfall said. "Cal had talked her into getting a test because she was coughing. She had quit smoking years ago. They found something. Now she has to have more tests."

"There are false positives all the time, "Willie said.

"She looks all right to me ," Steve said.

"She's been good since she moved here," Waterfall said. " But you don't know the hell she had to go through to get here. When my father went to jail we lost every-thing. We started the surf business from jewelry she sold that she had hidden from the lawyers. "

"Waterfall was the first East Coast Surfing Champion," Steve told her. "Willie brags on you all the time, but he never mentions your sex life.I need to know."

"Sometimes, you are such an asshole," Waterfall said. "We used to go visit my father in prison. He was writing his appeal. I had to smuggle it out on toilet paper hid-den in my bra. Mother would type it up when we got home. After five years, his conviction was over-turned. The Court ruled that the prosecution had knowingly used perjured testimony to convict him. And they were warned against ever trying to prosecute him again without being charged with criminal conduct."

"What was he charged with?" Steve asked.

"Selling worthless swampland," Willie said.

"In the Everglades," Steve asked.

"No," Waterfall said. "What is now Cape Canaveral. Indian River where all those houses are now. They knew they didn't have a good case, so they got a guy who bought one of the lots to say that Jack threatened to tell his boss that he was queer because he wanted his money back. That was extortion. Even though the guy told the judge that that didn't scare him because everybody knew he was gay. But the newspaper called my father the Al Capone of Florida and the jury only knew that he owned a lot of property even though it was all mortgaged to the hilt. My father never threatened him and that's what he told the prosectors, but one of them was a lawyer who my father fired for incompetence who became a prosecutor and saw a chance to get back at him. Eventually two of the prosecutors were made judges and convicted of extorting sex from victims and the woman was caught having sex with a felon in her car. Justice prevailed."

"Innocent Man Finally Freed," Willie said. "I have the screen rights."

"The only things he saved was that hundred acres near Lake Okeechobee," Waterfall said. "We were pioneers. We cleared the land, put in roads..."

"I put in the wells," Willie said. "It was easier than selling women's shoes in my father's store."

"My father gave mother and I our own block of lots that we developed and we live off the income now. It built this house." Waterfall said.

"We lived in a single wide trailer with two kids and the white faced dog the kids brought home," Willie said. "On three hundred dollars a month and the money Waterfall brought in by selling her art work at festivals around the state."

"It was peanuts," Waterfall said," But we ate a lot of peanuts."

"I lived in an apartment in Manhatten and hid money for large corporations overseas," Steve interrupted.

"It's always about you," Waterfall teased. "Where's the money?"

"You always get to the point," Steve said.

11.

They moved down the path into the dunes in a small valley surrounded by sea oats. Nothing was heard from the house nor the beach but the sound of the surf. Steve spoke slowly.

"We are the Credit Suisse Investment Bank of the Cayman Islands." He smiled and put his arms out inclusively.

" There was this big white building down near the dock where the cruise ships come in. Outside was this big wall full of nameplates. All banks. And there was a stationary store in the lobby where I got our letterhead made. I showed you that letter of credit from our bank saying that we have the thirty million in an account for Ernest Hemingway's The Fifth Column."

"Who signed the letter?" Waterfall asked.

"Frangis," Steve said. " Mister Frangis to you. He works for us. He's the head of the bank. He's our gay assistant. Everybody in show business has a gay assistant. You're going to ask if all this is legal."

"You read my mind," Waterfall said.

"Sounds like show business to me." Willie said.

"As your accountant and partner, " Steve said. "We have only created a financial entity. We haven't written any bad checks or borrowed any money. People with money only give money to people who don't need money. That's us. We are fully funded."

" But it doesn't mean any thing until we get the call from Alfred Rice, with Mary's signature." Willie said.

"He'll call," Steve said. "After all no one else is knocking at his door. Isn't that what he said when he agreed to take seven grand for the play. Dramatist Guild standard contract"

"He said he's not holding an auction," Willie said. "And Mary agreed. He just had to get her to sign the contract, but she wasn't feeling well. He had an appointment to see her today and he'd take the contract with him. He said he would call as soon as the ink dried."

"Maybe she's dead," Steve said, "and he just has her pen."

"I 'll be in the water," Waterfall said and headed up over the dunes. The two men followed. A sea breeze blew away some of the heat of the day but the sand was still hot.

Both men wore brief bathing suits and were physically fit. Steve was the darker and shorter of the two, his semetic ancestry dominant. There was a bounce in his step and a smile on his face. Willie was more the white Russian with unruly brown hair and thick legs. His steps were heavier. The contrast between the two was obvious to the eye, but their similarities were more important.

They were both third generation Jews with relatives in a small Russian town Kovne Gabernia. The were within a year of each other in their forties and therefore had a common frame of reference from two northeastern cultures, though Willie had now spent half of his life a Floridian.

They had met at a small airport in Jacksonville where Steve was doing accounting work in exchange for flying lessons and teaching accounting at a Business College.

Willie and Waterfall had come by with Gerard Fiore, a French pilot from the island of Saint Barths who needed to learn English so he could get an International License to start an air cargo service to import food from the larger islands.

Willie and Waterfall met him when they were living in Saint Barth's spending the money they got from renting out their large downtown house. They had rented an apartment Gerard owned on top of a hill overlooking Bay St. Jean. They were so comfortable there that they let their eleven year old daughter hitchhike down the hill to buy bread and ham.

When Gerard asked if he could stay with them at their downtown

house and learn English and teach
them French they accepted without
hesitation. He was a gentleman
and a comic, a former world class
skier who had blown out both
knees on a sixty foot drop. He also
cooked. Almost every night they
would sit in the hot tub and talk in
the two languages.

Willie and Waterfall took Gerard
to the small airfield for flying lessons in English and where they first
met Steve. The head of the flight
school wanted to fix Gerard up
with a Norwegian instructor. Steve
stepped in to remind the boss that
they had in their services Maxalon
Decort, the youngest female commercial pilot in France. They all be-

came friends and partied at Steve's place on the weekends.

It was the beginning of a long friendship.

CHAPTER THREE

12.

Willie accompanied Gerard on his final check ride for his license in English. The man who was to judge him had a southern accent so thick Willie couldn't understand half of what he said.

"This ain't gonna be no Sunday school picnic," the Inspector told Gerard.

Gerard looked at Willie and his jaw dropped.

There was a moment in the check ride when the instructor directed Gerard to make a left turn over the International Airport. Gerard wouldn't do it . The Inspector insisted. Gerard looked at Willie in the back seat and down to the left. A large commercial airliner was lifting off the runway and a turn would have resulted in a disaster.

The Inspector was writing in his exam book and shaking his head before he looked at Gerard and said.

"This just ain't gonna make it."

In perfect English Gerard said, "Sir, did you not see that airplane you were directing me to hit." He looked back at Willie as his witness. Willie shook his head. Gerard passed his test and got his license . Now all he needed was an airplane.

They found a Cherokee Six that was perfect for the short runway in Saint Barths. Gerard bought blue ice that he would use for carrying lobsters.It was a blue liquid in a plastic sacks about two liters. After being kept in a freezer it would solidify and say cold longer than water.

Willie agreed to accompany Gerard when he took the plane down island to his home. He was to help him with his English, the language used internationally for communication.

The first stop was to be the Bahamas. They looked down at the busy sea lanes as they flew over the deep dark blue Gulf Stream. That's when the engine failed and the nose dropped down. Willie reached under seat for his life jacket and a fishing knife he carried. Gerard quickly switched over to the second fuel tank and the they were flying again. Gerard looked at Willie and laughed pointing to the knife.

"For the sharks," Gerard said. He was comic. Willie put the life jacket back under the seat. He put the knife on his belt.

As they were approaching the airport their radio broke. They were within sight of the runway but lost contact with the tower.

Gerard looked at Willie for an answer.

There were scattered clouds and as they descended through one they saw a commercial air liner approaching ; a near miss. Gerard dove down and turned away and they were in another cloud unable to see anything. They broke out below and saw the jet liner land. They looked at the air space above around and below.

"a le pist," Willie said in bad French. "The runway before another plane comes in."

The landing was swift and smooth. Willie had flown with Gerard many times as his interpreter when he was shopping for a plane. There had been so many takeoffs ands landings that Willie would fall asleep in the back seat. They taxied past a long line of planes with flat tires.

"Those are the ones they seized in drug busts," Willie said.

They parked the plane in an open spot at the end of the line and prepared to check in at customs. As the were getting out of the plane two jeeps with unformed men carrying guns pulled up beside them.

"Only speak in French," Willie told Gerard.

"Bon jour, " Gerard smiling said and stuck out his hand to greet the first man to approach.

The man held back his hand and placed it on the handle if the gun he had around his waist. The other men surrounded the plane and watched intently. Two of the men had machine guns.

"We lost our radio," Willie said. "We had an emergency landing and we want to check in with customs."

One of the officers had circled the plane and opened the front storage compartment. He pulled out two plastic bags of blue ice. He held them up for the senior member to see.

"Cocaine !" the man said.

"No!"Willie said. "Blue ice! Blue ice!"

"Blue ice," Gerard said. "For flying lobsters."

"What kind flying lobsters," the man laughed and hefted the sack of blue ice in his hands. "Mon, who do you think you're talking to a fool?"

"Only French," Willie whispered to Gerard and then addressed the policeman. "He is comic. There are no flying lobsters. He uses his plane to fly fresh lobster into Saint Barths where he lives."

The cop smiled and handed the blue ice to one of his subordinants. He looked at Willie in his shorts and tee shirt. He pointed to the knife Willie had strapped to his belt. Willie carefully removed it and handed ot over to the cop. They both smiled.

"Come with me," the cop said and turned his back and walked over to one of the escort vehicles.

They followed and got in the back of a van with two men who carried automatic rifles.

The police headquarters was a nondescript stucco building with a large counter inside and an old leather couch across from it where two men half dressed in police uniforms sat. Behind the counter a large man in police pants and a tee shirt pulled on a heavey blue uniform jacket. He pulled up his pants over a large belly and tightened his belt. There was a gun on his hip.

"Cocaine," the arresting officer declared and tossed the evidence onto the counter. The man behind the counter looked at Willie and Gerard. He buttoned up his jacket, pulled in his gut and tightened his belt. His right hand rested on the butt of the gun.

" We have to go over to the office and clear customs and find a way to get our radio fixed," Willie said ignoring the evidence. "He's French and he's taking his plane ..."

"So, you are the guys," the chief said. "You almost hit an airliner. They be looking for you." He looked at the evidence sack on the counter. "Blue ice. I use it at the beach. Cool runnen."

He looked at the arresting officer who was grinning and exchanging glances with the two men on the couch. The three of them went outside and could be heard laughing. The chief shook his head and smiled .

"Where do we check in?" Willie asked.

The chief looked at a clock on the wall. "It's too late now. Everything is closed down. You'll have to wait until tomorrow."

Willie and Gerard slept in their plane.

They had to jump through hoops, swear allegiance, sign their names and promise to never do it again. In the meantime Willie contacted the people who sold Gerard the plane and they promised to replace the radio if he would return to the Opa Locka Airport where he bought it. They were ready to file a flight plan and go back to Florida.

The man at the desk was ready for them. He greeted them with a big smile. "So, you're the two blue ice smugglers !"

Gerard was a mimic. If he was walking down the street and saw someone with a different stride, he would go behind them and imitate their movements. He looked at the man behind the counter, pulled in his stomach and hitched up his imaginary belt and rested his hand on his imaginary gun. The man behind the counter burst out laughing.

"I know who you mean," he caught his breath. "You didn't clear customs because you weren't allowed to enter the country. So, I'm not sure you can file a flight plan out of here."

"Doesn't everybody have to file a flight plan?" Willie asked.

"They should, but most of these guys file a flight plan and then change it once they get in the air," he nodded to the long line of flat tired planes out on the field.

Since they had no radio, arrangements had been made with the Opa Locka tower that they would approach from the east and circle the tower where they would be signaled with a red or green light as to when to land. It was a short flight. As soon as they reached altitude they were able to see the Florida coast. They found the small airport on their heading just after they flew over the pastel water and hotels along the coast. One time around the tower and they got the green light. To the south of them a larger plane was approaching but they were far ahead of it as they began their approach and descent onto the runway.

As they were about to touch down they saw a fire engine and an ambulance heading directly for them.

"They must see something we can't," Willie said .

"No radio," Gerard shrugged.

"The landing gear."

"Is good?"

They braced as the wheels touched and the vehicles came head on and then past them. Willie and

Gerard laughed. They could not see what was behind them.

They taxied over near the customs office and went inside. The officer was smoking a cigar and leafing through paperwork. He smiled at them.

"What's going on?" Willie asked.

"Emergency landing," he said. "Passenger plane going to Puerto Rico."

"This is a long way from Puerto Rico," Willie said.

"They changed their flight plan once they were in the air." he said and Willie and Gerard looked at each other.

A big silver twin engine cargo plane that had been converted for passengers pulled up outside the office. A small black helicopter flew in and landed next to it. A Sherrif's car pulled up and a local police car with two men came too. As Willie and Gerard went outside to watch, an old Ford Station wagon with four men in street clothes pulled up next to a dumpster next to the building.

A stairway was rolled up next to the plane and a stewardess opened the rear door. A man in a black uniform and two police officers were up the steps and inside. A second woman in a stewardess outfit carried two large black trash bags out onto the steps.

"If I don't get this garbage off the plane it will be full of roaches in the morning," they could hear her say as she came down the steps. She took the two bags of garbage and set them on the ground next to the dumpster and went back to the plane. The four men in street clothes picked up the black bags and threw them into the back of the Ford station wagon and they got in and drove away. Gerard looked at Willie.

"Blue ice ?"he said.

They jumped through the hoops, the I swears and promised to never do it again. Gerard got a new radio and decided to fly by way of Cuba. He could do that. He was French. Willie went back home.

CHAPTER FOUR

13.

They walked with their capes wrapped around them against the wind. The hoods were pulled up over their ears where the wind whistled. It blew swirling sand devils across the beach and into the dunes.

The tide was out. With pants rolled up they would dip bare feet into the sea, water that was warmer than the air and earth. A dense fog drifted in and out hiding the horizons. The dogs ran ahead and disapeared in the mist.

"They think he's living off of you,"the Contessa said. They were shoulder to shoulder, looking like reflections of each other. She didn't know if Waterfall had heard her. Her daughter's face was straight into the wind, her eyes squited against gusts of sand. It was her idea to walk out against the wind and return with the wind behind them.

"He's Gerard's American agent so they can import internationally. I don't know all the details." Waterfall said. "First they need to get the plane to Saint Barths. I have nothing to do with it."

"He could be sued,"the Contessa thought out loud.

"He doesn't care," Waterfall said. "He doesn't own anything."

"He's with Gerard right now," Waterfall said. "He's his interprter."

"Willie speaks French?"the Contessa said

"Poorly," Waterfall laughed, "enough to find a bathroom or a meal"

"Is Gerard paying him?"

"He's buying his ticket home."

The wind had blown the clouds past them and they could see the beach ahead of them and the dunes. The sea was still clouded in a muffled roar. The wind let up.

The two dalmations were chasing fish in the tideline while the black dog walked beside them. The Dane was making great strides straight ahead. In the dunes a large woman with a small dog was coming on a pathway from a house hidden in fog. The small dog yapped in front of her.

When the Dane heard the barking dog, she changed course and ran to the sound of the barking. The woman saw the Dane coming at a gallop and she threw her body down over her dog covering it completely in a protective shell. The Dane stopped, sniffed, and hopped around like she wanted to play. When there was no response, she lost interest and continued back to her path.

As the two capes passed their faces were hidden in the hoods and silent. The large woman glared at them as she picked up her pooch then faded out back where she came from.

"Leash law," Waterfall warned.

The wind increased. They pushed on. Their goal was to reach the watertower that was a mile from the house. This was their routine since before the first piling had been placed to begin the beach house. It had been years and generations. They walked this mile to-gether. Sometimes the Contessa walked it with her dogs in the eve-ning. The beach was wide and the sky was endless. And the colors. Rainbows and starburst reflected in the water. Then way off across the sea a black line formed and grew into a curtain and she was able to run back to the house with her dogs, up the steps and undercover on her deck.

"Maybe we passed it," the Con-tessa coughed.

"Let's turn around," Waterfall said.

With the wind behind them it was easier to breath with lowered voices. The dogs soon found them and raced "back to the barn." Only the black dog stayed with them. She had a white face that had once been full black when they found her. That was when they lived in the country before the Contessa built the beach house. The black dog had grown old with Waterfall's family. Now she had retired to the beach where one day she would walk off into the dunes and never return.

"Do you trust this guy Steve?"the Contessa asked. " He seems a bit crooked to me."

"Willie won't do anything illegal," Waterfall said. "They've got big plans after Mary Hemingway signs that contract. Steve is taking us to Cannes for the film festival once we have the movie rights.

Steve is the most generous person I know."

"It all sounds pretty shakey to me,'the Contessa said.

" If they've got a signed contract, "Waterfall said. "What can go wrong?"

"Ask your father about that,"the Contessa whispered.

"They never liked him did they," Waterfall said.

They walked with ease and the wind. All resistance was gone. Emotions relaxed without bias or predudice.

"Who?"the Contessa said.

"Your family," Waterfall said. "My uncles and aunties."

"He was a farm boy and they were all college professors," the

Contessa said. "He didn't fit in and then he had that legal trouble. They were all happy when we got divorced."

"But not completely seperated,"

"We have so many things entangled,"the Contessa said.

"He's getting it all straightened out. Just feel the air."

She breathed deeply and held back the cough.

They both waded down to the water and splashed along until they came to a white thing protruding from the sand. They stopped. The sea was always washing up treasures. They looked at the finger sized object. With their capes held between their legs, they bent down to inspect. They moved the sand away and it widened to hand size.

They looked at each other as a wave washed in around it, and they dug faster as it ran out. Waterfall reached down and grabbed a flat surface below the hand and pulled up. It came loose with a strong smell of putrafication that the wind quickly dispersed. There was something long dead deeper down. She handed it to her mother who was nearer the sea to wash it off.

"Turtle," Waterfall said, taking the flat pointed rib.

"I thought we were going to find a body,"the Contessasa laughed.

The wind had lessened and the fog had lifted. They looked toward the dunes. Ahead they could see the morning sun reflected in the windows of the beach house.

This was a god day.

There had been bad days when the chemo started. But her mother was imporoving. Thank God.

"Without faith," the Contessa said. "There is no hope."

Waterfall had faith that she was cured. She hoped that she would not have to go through it again. She had no idea how she had taken care of the vomit, the blood and the shit. The stench.

The Contessa had these good days now when no one would believe that there had been days so bad that Waterfall and the Contessa wished she was dead. They got through it with the bell.

The bell. When the Contessa needed help there was a small bell on her night table next to her bed in one of the rooms off of the hallway. Waterfall had moved into the room on the upper floor. It had a king size bed with room enough for Willie when he stayed with her. She could hear the bell even with the door closed.

During the day, a nurse came to help. The nights belonged to Waterfall. Standing on the walkover to the beach, not too far from the house, she could hear the bell. She inhaled the sea in the distance thinking of clear water and colorful reefs. She wished that she was back on the boat. Getting back to the boat was feeling safe . Safe from all the troubles and turmoil on the land.

Willie was fixing the diesel engine again in Key West but came up on weekends. The girls were both away at school. Waterfall had the duty all night.

"He fixes things?" the Contessa said.

"Yes," Waterfall said.

"That's not what Cal said," the Contessa scoffed. "He screwed up my outside light."

"You just don't know how to work it." Waterfall was defensive. " Cal is full of shit."

"That's no way to talk about your brother," the Contesssa defended her son.

"You always defend him," Waterfall said. "Even when we were kids. He used to beat me up and when I told you about it, you ignored me."

"You were the older one," the Contessa said.

"You'd always say that," Waterfall said. "After school I would run away and hide in a tree until you got home. At night I would hide and wait for you and Dad. But you two would always come in screaming at one another about a stupid play at bridge or a bad bet at the track."

"I don't want to talk about it," the Contessa said.

"You're right," Waterfall said. She didn't want to upset her on a good day. But soon the night would come and she would hear the bell. It was a signal for resposibility and capability. Waterfall had both but they were wearing thin. She realized that her mother was dieing. But, when?

"I'm feeling much better since they stopped the radiation,"the Contessa said. "Soon you'll be able to go back to your house at night. I want my room back. Your father said he was coming up and Captain Mark is coming."

14.

The Contessa sat in her car in the driveway. It was a Mercedes diesel that had a rattle and emitted big puffs of black smoke from time to time. She pressed the horn and it squacked. She pressed it again. She liked the sound. She had been waiting a lot lately. Exams, consultations and the next guy. But this time she knew what she was waiting for.

She was waiting for her daughter and her two granddaughters. She turned off the ignition and the rattle stopped. She looked up through the trees in the front yard.

There was a vivid red cardinal. She closed one eye so she could see better.

Behind the bird was the large two story mansion that Waterfall had bought at a bargain when the rest of the neighborhood was run down. It was the best house on the block. It was four big bedrooms so that everybody had one. Sometimes they would switch and a guest room became a studio or an office.

She got out of the car and straightened her silk dress that she had ironed that morning. She was colorfully stylish and her handbag matched her white shoes. Her underwear was new. Her skin was eternally golden smooth and hair-

less from some oriental roots that
led back to Marco Polo going to
China. Her hair was wavey white.
It had once been black. The girls
had done her nails the night before.
They were red and matched her lipstick. She was beautiful. She had
always been beautiful and would
be til the day she died. She didn't
feel bad. Why should she look bad.
She was ready to check into the
hospital and they were all coming
with her; her "precious jewels."

"I'm sitting in the back,"the Contessa yelled. "somebody else drive."

They came out the front door as
flowers blosseming in the air. They
were all adults now, but to her they
were still children. Both girls, Rita
and Sophia were in college now at

different ends of the country but
they were back home now because
they wanted to be there for her.
They still had their rooms in the big
house. The Contessa liked the
house but she liked hers a lot more.
She was longing to be back with her
dogs and her cocktail on her deck
looking out to sea and breathing in
the fresh sea air.

The flowery maidens flew into
the car. Waterfall sat in back with
her mother. The two girls sat up
front and the eldest drove.

"Where's your father?" the Contessa asked.

"He's waiting for a call from
New York," the youngest said.
"Somebody wants him to produce a
play about old people."

"Old people!" the Contessa said. "What does he know about old people?"

"You told him that every day after you reach forty," Waterfall said. "You find another ache or pain."

"I never," the Contessa said.

"Yes you did," Sophia said. "I heard you. He calls it your Italian curse on him."

"It was on his birthday," Rita said.

" I was only joking," the Contessa said. " You know that's why Marilyn Monroe killed herself. She turned forty."

The Contessa thought about aches and pains but she wouldn't let it bother her. She didn't feel sorry for living to be an old person.

A Senior. That's what they called her now. If she died from the cancer, it was okay. Her life had been full. She had been good to others all of her life. She had no enemies. She had nothing to confess. She just didn't want any pain.

If Cal hadn't tricked her into getting that check up she would be watching the dolphins rounding up mullet off shore.

CHAPTER FIVE

15.

"It was like looking down from the top a cliff," Waterfall was telling Steve, when Willie finished up in the shower wiping himself with a large pink, white and blue stripped towel.

"That's Captain Mark's towel," Waterfall said.

"He gave it to me for my birthday," Willie said.

"Captain Mark, the hero who saved the Contessa's life?" Steve said.

"Waterfall saved her mother's life" Willie corrected him.

"It was a team effort," Waterfall said.

They were sprawled in chairs on the deck in shady places when the Contessa, Auntie and Uncle came out. Willie nodded hello and shook Uncle's hand. Steve was introduced and did the same. Uncle was showing more age and less hair. His blue polo shirt and tan shorts were correct for Florida. He wore leather flip flops.

"You're a bad girl !" Auntie accosted Waterfall. She was a mean old woman with deep lines in her face. Her hair was grey and combed and sprayed into place. She wore a short sleeve cotton dress and wedged sandals.

Waterfall was aways 'the bad girl'. Tomboy, barefoot, two children, unwed and a man who lives off of her.

" Leave her alone," the Contessa said.

"It's not the first time I've heard it," Waterfall said "The waves are so beautiful now, I think I'll go for a swim."

"Don't go out too far," the Contessa said.

"I know, I know, " Waterfall walked down to the sea.

"So, what do you do?" Uncle asked Steve.

" I'm a bookkeeper at an air-field," Steve was being civilized.

"Im retired, " Uncle said. "I worked for thirty years at the same company."

The Uncle ignored Willie. They had gotten along over the years talking about fishing and hard work. But when he and Waterfall had taken their younger daughter up to school at Harvard to study French and Journalism, they had spent the night at Uncle's house on the Cape. They were to ride back home with one of their daughter's girlfriends who was visiting her boyfriend. She asked if she could spend the night so they could get an early start in the morning. She was willing to sleep on the floor in the living room. She had a sleeping bag.

Uncle threw a fit. There wasn't enough food for an extra person. Who was the boyfriend? They'll be fornicating up against the walls. No. No. No.

"You're just waiting for her to die," Uncle told Willie. "So you can get your hands on this house."

"Thank God the children don't have that horrible southern accent, " Auntie said.

"Y'all come back real soon ya hear," Willie said and got up to go follow Waterfall.

Steve got up to follow Willie.

The dogs got up to see who was coming up the drive way.

"It's Captain Mark," the Contessa smiled.

16.

The Contessa owned a sixteen foot motor boat with the engine mounted on the back. It was an open boat with a bimini top and seats molded into the hull for eight people. They used it for fishing and trips up and down the river to dockable restaurants and distant beaches. She bought the boat back when Mark was in the Navy and he would come by on leave and he would take them out on the ocean. Nowadays he was working for Haliburten on boats all over the oil producing world. He had worked his way up to Captain on ships of unlimited tonnage. His boat now was "Buster" the largest ocean going tugboat in the world.

He was a boyish looking man with a sweep of blonde hair and rosy cheeks. He had gained a little weight since his Navy days but still was quick on his feet. However he drank and smoked too much and would eventually fall asleep in the middle of a sentence.

Captain Mark had been on a visit home from Bahrain in the Arabian Gulf in the middle of summer accompanied by a saluki, one of those skinny desert dogs that the Sheiks allowed in their tents because they didn't smell. The dog got off of his leash and ran down the beach. After chasing the dog for miles on the beach Mark had to get back out to sea so they took out the little runabout without the dog.

The dog's name was Sadek but Captain Mark called him "Shithead."

There was the Contessa, Waterfall and Willie in the seats while Captain Mark stood at the wheel. Mark took off his shirt so he could feel the sun on his white back. His arms from were tan up to the middle of his upper arm. He had a baseball cap pulled down almost to the bridge of his nose and a cigarette in his mouth and a beer can set in front of him next to the windshield.

As they headed out the inlet, the Contessa leaned forward to pick something off of Mark's back. She pulled at it with her finger nails and a sliver of fiberglass came out leaving a spot of blood. She dabbed at it with a towel. Mark winced but said nothing.

"What the hell was that?" Waterfall said.

"When I was in Viet Nam," Mark said without taking his eyes from his heading, " I was running a plastic boat up the river and an explosive round landed in the middle. Every once in a while another piece comes up."

"Didn't they take care of it at the hospital?" Willie said.

"They never get them all," Mark said. "I had to spend two nights in a tree along the bank before they picked me up. I wasn't hurt that bad. My crew all made it back."

Mark pulled on the cigarette and drank some beer with one hand on the wheel. He guided them out the channel and leaned forward on the throttle as they headed out against the incoming swells moving into the river from the sea. They put the Bimini top down and held onto the sides of the boat until they got out beyond the shoals where the water was calm. Mark steered out beyond the breakers to the south and they ran parallel to the beach about a mile offshore. The sun was bright, the beer was cold and the roll of the sea was rhythmic and steady.

"There's my house," the Contessa sprang up from her seat in the stern pointing to the distant A frame set high above the dunes. A few miniature people and toy sized cars could be seen on the beach.

Captain Mark throttled back and turned toward the land riding the rollers until they were just outside where the waves were breaking over the first sandbar.

"It's hot out here," the Contessa said. "I'm going to swim to my house. I'll have dinner ready by the time you get back."

She took off her hat and sunglasses and the long sleeve shirt that she wore over her bathing suit.

"Are you crazy?" Waterfall said to her mother.

"Look how close we are,"the Contessa said. "I grew up on the Cape. I've been swimming since I was five years old. Mark, turn around so I can hop off the back."

Mark took a long sip on his beer turned the wheel until they were facing away from the beach, shifted into neutral and the propeller stopped spinning. Waterfall tried to grab her mother but it was too late. Willie watched as the Contessa stepped over the transom and plopped into the water.

Distances at sea are deceptive. Five miles can look like a hundred yards. From the top of a swell you can see the faces of the people on shore and if the wind is right you can even hear the children laughing in the surf and music from portable players. Then the wave rolls under you and drops you into the trough and the only thing you can see is the sea and the only sound you can hear is your own heartbeat as you realize how insignificant you are.

The Contessa began to swim and then she began to cough and turned onto her back and waved both arms.

"She's in trouble," Waterfall said and was over the side before Willie and Mark heard the splash.

"Let's go get her," Captain Mark said as calmly as if he were asking for another beer. "Willie, get on the stern. "I'll put us next to her. You pull her aboard." There was no sound of danger in his voice but his eyes were wide and his movements were controlled.

The Contessa was spitting with only her head above the water. Waterfall swam along side her and got an arm under her neck while treading water. The sea had moved them closer to the sandbar and the crash of the waves was louder than the boat's motor.

Captain Mark steered the boat while watching for the next set of waves measuring the distance between them. He maneuvered so the back of the boat drifted to the women and he shifted the boat into neutral so they would not be injured by the propeller. Willie leaned over the transom and Waterfall pushed the Contessa up from underwater. He grabbed the Contessa's hand as she reached for him. His other arm went over her back and grabbed the seat of her bathing suit, anchoring himself to the deck with his feet his knees braced against the hull. They could feel the rise of the incoming wave. As the boat rose up with the help of the sea Willie pulled up hard as the wave began to break. Captain mark put the boat in gear and pushed forward on the throttle as they drove down the back of the wave and the Contessa came up over the transom and sprawled on top of Willie as he fell backward to the deck.

Captain Mark turned in a half circle until they could see Waterfall go over the falls as the wave broke and tossed her into the white water where she disappeared. She surfaced with a smile on her face and a wave of her hand. With a turn as smooth as a dolphin she raised one leg. She turned onto her belly and swam to shore.

"She'll be okay," Willie said. "We've come out farther than this before."

"She was on the swim team in high school," the Contessa coughed out her words. She reached behind and pulled her swimsuit out of her buttocks and sat up on one of the seats. She composed herself and held back on the coughing. "Please let me have a sip of your beer."

Captain Mark handed her the can without taking his eyes from the water as he headed away from the beach. She took a long cold sip and breathed easy. She threw her head back and took a long deep breath inhaling life.

"I didn't realize it was so far, " she said. "I got out of breath so fast.

I don't know how you kept the whole boat from going over. You're a life saver."

" You should try it in fifty foot swells with a sixty knot wind blowing the top off the waves and green water on the deck," Captain Mark said. " We were towing a barge full of supplies for an oil platform in the Arab Gulf and the tow line breaks and you have to cut the tow line to survive and you have to go back and pick up the barge when the weather passes. Willie, could you hand me another cerveza por favor?"

CHAPTER SIX

17.

Waterfall had the pasta boiling and the sauce started.

"You saved my life," the Contessa told her as they worked together in the kitchen.

"It was Captain Mark," Waterfall said. "Did you see the way he handled your boat. He saved us all."

"I couldn't have made it," the Contessa said." I was down to my last breath and I knew it."

"I had you all the way," Waterfall said. "When you jumped in I knew I was going to have to go in after you and besides Willie and Mark know CPR."

"Cut up this onion," the Contessa changed the subject and Waterfall was quiet.

When Waterfall was swimming in from the boat a rogue wave came under her and lifted her to it's crest. She looked down the face of the wave and felt as if she were standing on the edge of a cliff. She tried to back off but the top of the wave caught her and tossed her over the falls and down into the sandbar, being rolled in the wave over and over until there was no up, only sand and water. Then suddenly bottom and a path to the sky and she thrust to the surface, grabbed a quick breath before the next set crashed upon her. She was caught in the vortex of the third wave that brought her up in it's curl. She was able to look down the tunnel of rolling water to the shrinking glow of the horizon. She quickly stretched her arms in front of her and rode the white water to the shore.

They continued to work side by side in the kitchen. It wasn't the first time. They were a team.

"Where are the partners ?" the Contessa strained the pasta and Waterfall poured the sauce from the pan into a large blue bowl.

"They're in the garage with Captain Mark, " Waterfall said. "Something about an electrical problem."

The famiglia sat at the table inside. Places were set for six. A large wooden mahogany bowl was set in the middle of the table. The Contessa prepared plates with pasta and sauce and Waterfall served. They knew the garlic bread was done when they smelled it burning.

The "boys" came up from the garage. They all carried a look of disappointment.

"I thought you were going to make that fish," the Contessa said.

"It's on the grill, "Willie said pointing to the side door opposite the entrance where the deck wrapped around and caught the afternoon sun sheltered from the afternoon sea breezes.

"Let's eat out on the deck," Waterfall said.

"They don't know how to eat at a table," the Contessa said.

Willie was commanding the grill on the side deck cooking the shark while Captain Mark told Steve about his arrest in Nigeria. He had steaked out the fish and set it in a bowl of milk to purify. He had emptied the liquid and was squeezing on some lemon and olive oil. He had a special datil pepper sauce that he got from Cecil at the Devil's Elbow Fish camp.

Cecil made the best smoked mullet. He always scraped out the bitter black lining of the stomach and covered it in his sauce. Cecil always said the secret was in the sauce. And he never revealed that secret.

Down the road from Cecil's was Phil Cochran's where Willie and Waterfall would go for fresh local seafood and the best local raw oysters. They had a sweetness and the taste of the sea. Willie and Waterfall would each get a pint of raw oysters. They would buy crackers, hot sauce and a couple of beers at the 7/11. They had an orange Volkswagon beach buggy with a rag top that was easy to put down. Then they would drive down to the beach and eat the oysters on crackers with a dab of hot sauce. They hardly spoke, only uttering sounds of delight . The liquor of the oysters ran over their lips that they wiped with their tongues.

The beach was usually empty in months with an "r" in them, the months it was safe to eat oysters. The blue sky had scattered clouds and lines of pelicans going in both directions. Seagulls and terns picked food out of the sand at the water's edge. The sea was a constant roll of blue and white.

The coals on the grill were red hot and the fish sizzled as it hit the grate. The shark had no bones, only cartilage which was easy to slice and dissolved if cooked right. Fast and Hot.

"Willie, you're a master," Steve said admiring Willie's technique with the tongs. "Captain Mark look at his movements. "

" Is there enough light to work down there at night?" Mark asked.

"Sure, " Willie said. "We can always rig up some of Waterfall's camera lights. We have all the tools."

"Tools for what?" Waterfall said coming around the corner of the deck. "An electrical problem?"

"Tools for diving a treasure ship," Willie said.

"Diving !" Waterfall said. "You wouldn't even know how to dive if it wasn't for me."

"And you wouldn't be able to tell that story if it wasn't for me."

"Mon hero," Waterfall said. "I could have kicked my way to the top."

They had been diving off the Juno wall, a coral cliff full of life that dropped off at seventy feet down to one hundred and ten feet and ran for miles near the Gulf stream. Most of the colors faded at that depth because of the filtered light. The red blood of a speared fish became a green mist. An orange starfish was grey on the sand.

The Rapture of the Deep or nitrogen narcosis can begin at seventy feet and the deeper one goes the more likely the effect will occur. If you are aware of the drunkenness it brings, you can overcome it by concentrating on air gauge, depth gauge, timer. You can live with it or if you don't know it's there you run out of air and die.

"I didn't want to come up," Waterfall said. "Willie showed me my air gauge and all I wanted to do was swim into that incredible wall."

"I had to grab her and inflate her vest to get her to go up," Willie said. "And we had to flare so we wouldn't go up too fast and get an embolism."

"And I was fighting him the whole way," Waterfall said. "I didn't want to go up."

"She was mad as hell when we surfaced and she was yelling and calling me names," Willie said. "Then as we were bobbing there drifting toward the boat. I showed her her air gauge. It was on empty. So was mine. We came up on fumes."

" It was scary," Waterfall said.

"It's always about you," Steve said. "Captain Mark was just about to tell us about Nigeria. The cook killed the Captain."

"No, " Mark said . "That was in the Gulf at Bahrain. That's how I got to be Captain. And he was a good cook too."

"Willie," the Countessa call from inside, " There is someone on the phone for you. He said he's Alfred Rice."

Willie and Steve went inside.

"After we eat, " Mark said. "We can go down to the garage and take care of that electrical problem."

"You mean that crate that mother received for you," Waterfall said. "What's in it ?"

"My motorcycle, " Mark said.

"So what's the problem?"

"We have to take it apart."

"Is it broken?" Waterfall was watching the grill using a pair of tongs to turn the shark steaks until they were brown and slightly burned. She then placed them on a large green platter. She picked a piece of shark from a finished steak with her fingertips, blew on it to cool it and popped it into her mouth. She smiled.

"It's not broken, " Mark said. "But I bought a pound of red hashish when I was in Egypt and it's hidden in one of the cylinder heads."

Waterfall nearly choked on the shark and grabbed Mark's beer and swigged it.

Willie and Steve came out the side door. They were both grinning. They had their arms around each other's shoulder.

"Mary signed the contract," Willie said.

"We go to New York next week to give him some money and sign the contract," Steve said.

"I love New York," Willie said.

"My kind of town," Steve said. "'Your money or your life isn't a threat. It's a negotiation."

18.

Everyone sat around the large wooden table on the deck. The Uncle, Aunt and brother sat together. Steve sat at one end and kept everybody amused with jokes he had accumulated while traveling all over the world hiding money for a Fortune 500 company in New York. Willie and Waterfall shared a lounge chair and ate from trays on their laps.

"They don't know how to eat at a table," the Contessa said.

Captain Mark came out with a beer in his hand and a cigarette. As soon as the Contessa saw him, she waved to him to put it out.

" My brother Eddie never smoked a cigarette in his life. But he worked in a Casino in Las Vegas for forty years. He died of lung cancer. Second hand smoke."

Captaine Mark wet the end of the joint with his fingers and placed the remains in his shirt pocket.

"Sit over here, " the Contessa said. She slid over at her place at the head of the table. She prepared a plate for him.

"I have to get in the water ," Mark said. "I've been on land for too long. I have to get back to my mother, the sea."

"Fifty, a hundred thousand dollar in cash," Steve was telling his audience. "I was a smuggler."

"Don't tell anybody, " Waterfall said, "but Aunties smuggled diamonds out of Switzerland in her bra."

"You're a bad girl," Auntie said.

"Willie," the Contessa said. "Why don't you make us all some coffee."

"And my brother smuggled money out of Italy inside his down vest, "Waterfall told Steve. "So you should feel right at home." She followed Mark down to the sea.

The sea had calmed down in the afternoon. The shore break was a ripple that rolled up their backs as Waterfall and Captain Mark lay on their stomachs at the shoreline facing the dunes with the sea oats standing still blocking the view of the houses further inland. The sky to the west was filled with mountainous clouds rising until they flattened into anvils that promised rain somewhere to the west.

"Do you read the clouds ?" Waterfall asked him.

"I read the radar," Mark said.

"When we're on the boat," Waterfall said. "Willie is always watching the clouds. We don't have radar. Sometimes, he reads them wrong."

"I've been there," Mark said. "Sometimes even the radar reads them wrong. We were off the coast of Africa towing a platform to Nigeria when a storm came up behind us. The platform ran up onto my boat and we went down in those big rollers that come up from the cape. The crew got into a life raft and we set off the emergency beacon. I was the last one to leave the ship. I had on a dry suit that covered everything but my face but I was still cold and shivering until halfway through the night a rescue helicopter dropped a basket and pulled me out of the water."

"That's scary," Waterfall said. "The closest we came was off the Keys when we were hit by a rogue wave. Willie was down in the engine compartment putting out a fire. The compressor that ran off of the engine had come loose and was on a belt that pulled it into a bulkhead when we saw the smoke coming out of the aft cabin. I had to take the wheel while Willie went below. He cut the engine so he could cut the belt and we were drifting with only the jib and I tried to steer into the waves but the mizzen was still up and the wind kept turning us when I saw this huge wave off the starboard side. We broached. For the first time I can remember, that trimaran heeled over. But we righted ourselves and Willie came up and started the engine so we powered our way back to Big Pine Key. I was scared and Willie had gashed his head coming out of the engine room and had burned his hand. It was an adventure."

"You're a real sailor now," Captain Mark said.

"Because we lived ?" Waterfall asked.

"No," Captain Mark said. " Because you lived to tell the story."

They both laughed and rolled over to feel the sea wash over them.

"Tonight we can come down and get crabs, " Waterfall said.

"And we have the bottle rockets," Mark said.

Back at the house, Willie served the coffee to the folks at the table. The Aunt, the Uncle and the brother still sat together. The Contessa reclined on her chaise and Steve and Willie walked to the end of the deck where the dogs followed them.

"Get back," Willie said to the dogs and they went back and sat with the Contessa.

"What a great place this is, " Steve said.

"In the winter," Willie said, "I would come here to write while the Contessa was busy down south.

"Waterfall would take the dogs for a walk down on the beach and I'd sit up on the side deck with the southern exposure in the lee of the northers and write. The sun was warm even on the coldest days."

"Are you working on anything now?" Steve asked.

"You lose the writing when you talk about it," Willie said.

"Or you leave it in bed, Hemingway said," Steve added.

"I ran on the beach every day last year," Willie said."Then I'd go in for a dip no matter what the weather was. In the winter I ran south a mile and a half to the water tower and back. At the tower it was raining. As I ran back north to the beach house it turned to snow and a northeaster kicked up the waves to over six feet. Running back into the wind was a bitch, but if I leaned forward at the right angle I got lift and was flying. I still took my dip."

"I ran the New York City Marathon and came in ninety-ninth, " Steve said. "You think you're better than me?"

"Better than I," Willie corrected his grammar.

"Better than me am,"Steve said. "Better than I am. What's the difference? You know what I mean."

Willie didn't say anything. Standing on the end of the walkway he could see that the tide was out and Waterfall was still in the water while Mark sat further up the beach smoking a cigarette and sipping a canned beer that he had left up near the dunes.

"Is she as good as she looks in bed?"

He watched Waterfall for a while aware of what Steve was saying. He couldn't tell him what happened in their bed. There were some things not for publication. There was a right to privacy in the world of his mind that had no place in words. There were things so divine, so exquisite, so delicious that only the two of them shared.

CHAPTER SEVEN

19.

When Waterfall was a young girl she lived in Coconut Grove where she and her best friend Nora would sneak away to their hideout in a Banyan tree. It was a place where she was safe from the torment of her brother's abuse. An abuse that her parents refused to recognize.

When she returned to Coconut Grove with Willie, it was on a 41 foot trimaran, ketch rigged with a high center cockpit and a deck large enough to dance on. It was her refuge. It was her boat.

They were moored to a sunken engine block between two barrier islands just off the channel leading into Dinner Key marina. When the boat swung around with the tide, from the cockpit she could see the dinghy dock at Peacock Park. The masts of the boats in the basin could be seen above the top of the island. A canopy of green trees in the park obscured the pastel buildings on the mainland creating a jungle panorama like the one she grew up in. It hid the changes that had turned a small coastal village of artists and eccentrics into a suburb of high end shops, tourists and drug money; a bank on every corner and pushers pushed to the water's edge. A few homeless lived in the bushes and trees.

In the mornings, they would row the dinghy into the dock and walk to a small Cuban restaurant for coffee. They dressed in worn and weathered boat clothes as the homeless dressed and were not hustled by the vagrants when they came ashore. When they got back to the boat, they took a deep breath of freedom and looked back at the populace confined to the land.

They had no television and rarely read newspapers preferring to read the clouds and stayed tuned to the marine radio when they listened at all. They ate a lot of rice and beans, pasta and fresh vegetables when the cooler that ran off the engine was working. Willie spent a lot of time down below fixing and adjusting whatever needed to be fixed or adjusted. When they went ashore during the day it was usually to a marine supply store or the occasional palomia and plantains at the Cuban restaurant.

Some nights they walked the streets of the Grove. There   were some street artists they befriended and other mariners they met at happy hour buffets where they drank rum and sat at sidewalk cafes watching the parade of the well to do and too young to know better citizens who strutted their stuff, showed off their stuff and bought more stuff; some of it legal, some forbidden but all over priced. Then they returned to the sanctuary of the boat.

As much as she loved the sea, she loved the trees. They would walk along the tunnel of shade beneath the trees that lined Grand Highway. Waterfall would point out the hideouts that she had on her way home from elementary school. All of her life she seemed to be searching for a safe place. She and

Nora would climb high into the branches and look down on the world as it spun beneath them. She and Nora had cut their fingers, touched them together to become blood sisters. That was years ago and they had lost touch.

Willie had repaired the engine. Waterfall had gone to the top of the sixty foot mast in a boatswains chair to fix the wind gauge. He cranked her up using the mainsail winch. He then ran the video camera up on the pulley for the ship's flag so she could tape the adventure. She wasn't afraid of heights, but she was afraid of falling. The work took her mind off of her anxiety, and when it was done she didn't want to come down. The view was wonderful looking down at the tops of trees on the shore and away at the distant horizon where she knew they would soon be heading.

There was a small harbor across the bay in Crandon Park near the lighthouse. Boats would stop there for the night before they set out to cross the Gulfstream to the Bahamas. That would be their shake down cruise before they came back to the mooring and bought supplies for a longer voyage.

Waterfall was at the helm with the engine running while Willie unhooked from the mooring ball and locked the dinghy to it so that anyone would know that it was taken. The mainsail had already been raised flapping as she headed up into the wind. She turned off slightly as Willie unfurled the jib and both sails filled. The engine was running in neutral as they sailed out of the anchorage and headed across the bay. She cut the engine and the splash of the water against the hull could be heard. The wind picked up as they left the lee of the barrier islands that shielded the anchorage, the outer hulls slicing through the water as the main hull dipped and rose above the first swell of open sea.

There was a seawall around the small harbor, the lighthouse and a large motor yacht about to leave as they anchored and dropped the sails. On the aft deck of the yacht was a beautiful blonde woman taking in the morning sun. Ashore there was much activity and vehicles, cameras, lights and trailers. A movie was being made. The woman in the yacht was Faye Dunaway, easily recognized and they waved to her and she waved back in a grand gesture befitting her star quality.

"What movie is that?" Waterfall asked.

"I don't know," Willie said. "It doesn't look like Miami Vice."

"Lets swim ashore and go to the lighthouse," Waterfall said. "There's a stand there where we can get a drink and something to eat. We'll have to swim around the point to get to an open beach."

"Let me lock up," Willie said.

It was an easy swim in calm water. They wore billed caps and sunglasses taking their time after Waterfall dove to make sure the anchor was secure. They came up on the rough sand barefoot.

"When we were girls," Waterfall said. "We measured our fitness by the thickness of the callouses on our feet. We never wore shoes. Nora had big feet and bought her shoes at a men's store in Coral Gables."

They walked past the tall red brick lighthouse to a refreshment stand through a thicket of palm trees. There was a dark haired spanish girl who sold them cafe con leches and some sweet rolls called pastlitos. Behind the stand were some tables in the shade and a parking lot. They sat down at a table to dine. There was a jeep parked at one end of the lot.

"Nora loved nature," Waterfall said. "That's the kind of car she would drive."

A tall woman with a clipboard came out of the trees toward the jeep.

"Nora," Waterfall yelled.

"Waterfall," Nora yelled back and they ran to each other and embraced.

20.

"I saw Nora when we were in Miami," Waterfall told her mother as they walked along the beach with their frisbees in their hands. A threatening thunderstorm had sent Auntie, Uncle and brother on their way. Captain Mark, Steve and Willie were working on an electrical problem in the garage. The storm had passed to the south and the sky was taking on evening colors.

"Nora Denslow !" the Contessa said. "You're kidding ! After all these years. Does she still buy her shoes at the Men's store?"

They both laughed and watched the tide line as they searched for crabs. The Contessa got nipped first and yelped. She stooped down in the shallowest of water and then pounced with her frisbee splashing down on the crab. She slipped the frisbee under the crab and flipped it up onto the sand where Waterfall pinned it down with her frisbee then grabbed it at the back of the shell well behind the flailing pincers. With an outstretched arm she walked up the beach to where they had left a five gallon bucket and deposited the crab. It clattered around as Waterfall carried it nearer her mother who was holding another crab.

The Contessa stood in the shallows with her white pants rolled up. Her faded cotton shirt was pulled up to her elbows. Her tan face and arms and chest glowed in the fading light.

They walked and watched as the sea came in and out revealing two small eyes sticking above the sand as the water ran out where the crabs buried themselves. They would get in the water behind it and flip it with the frisbee, pin it, pick it up from behind and drop it in the bucket. They had to throw back the females if they had eggs. Waterfall got nipped and they both headed away with their bounty.

"Nora is a location scout for all the movies and tv that they make down their," Waterfall said. "It's because the light is so good. She still lives in that house near Colony Road. "

"After all these years!" the Contessa said. "We better get back to the house before those boys burn it down. What in the world are they doing down there?"

When they got to the ramp leading to the house they stopped. The A-frame was silhouetted against the pink and purple of the sky. They stopped while the Contessa caught her breath. Waterfall held her hand.

"I told them," the Contessa said. "Let them fight over it."

Waterfall didn't say anything.

"I have to make out a will," the Contessa said. "They want me to. I can't give you the house."

"What made you change your mind?" Waterfall asked.

"They said they didn't want Willie living in my house," the Contessa said. "You know how they feel about him not having a real job. And using your money to do a play."

"We don't need money," Waterfall said, "We're 'fully funded.' Just ask Steve."

They climbed the steps to the deck where the dogs were already laid out resting. They rinsed off their feet with a hose from the shower. They took the catch inside.

Inside, the Contessa's walls were covered with large paintings by her nephew Mario. He was a well known and respected artist who had made a living at his art for the last fifty years, after getting his start in the garage apartment of a house she and Jack owned in Coconut Grove. Quite a few from the art colony became famous in the sixties.

There was one painting that she and Jack had gotten from Mario years ago. It was an award winner.

Mario borrowed it for a show and they never got it back. It was an empty wall in her heart.

There was a photo of Jack getting a medal at a ceremony during World War II .

A large painting of the Contessa with a bird in her hair hung above the stairs. Waterfall had painted her coming out of the house in her red dress with a smile on her face. There was a large yellow sunflower in the background. She wore her Eva Peron ring and there was not a wrinkle on her face.

There were five of them around the table in front of the tall glass windows and doors. Steve blew kisses as he left to prepare for the trip to New York. The family' was long gone to the interstate. Before they left Cal hugged Waterfall.

"You're the greatest," he said. "For what you've done for mother." In the future he would be executor of the estate. Waterfall and her family would be banned from the beach house and it would be sold. She would never get the beach house.

Waterfall and Willie were taking crabs from a large steamer pot with large tongs and placing them on paper plates in front of everybody. The Contessa looked out at the colors of the sky. Captain Mark was nursing his sixth beer.

The sudden roar of the low flying jet thundered into the house shaking it enough to rattle dishes.

"That's probably an attack plane from the Saratoga," Mark said. His cheeks were rosey and his eyes were getting smaller as he leaned on his elbows feeling the cold of the bottle in his hand. "they're probably using the same plans that we used when I was on the Sara. We used to target the beach house because it was the only thing we could see when we had drills."

"So that's why those planes are always flying over the house," the Contessa said.

"Whenever the Sara is in Mayport," Mark said. "Yes, mam."

"You sighted on our beach house !" Waterfall shook her head. "What if someone accidently hit a button ?"

" Can't happen," Captain Mark said. "When we were in Bahrain, a couple of the crew got rousted in port and roughed up by the local police. When they got back to the ship, they went into a missile battery and targeted the palace of the local Sheik. They were going to fire but they needed power to energize the gun. When they asked engineering for juice, the Chief Gunny got suspicious and they were busted. They both live in Leavenworth now."

"Oh, my God," the Contessa said. "How stupid!"

"I've got some bottle rockets ," Captain Mark said and opened another beer.

"Not from my deck," the Contessa said.

Waterfall went inside to get the duffle bag Mark had left in the doorway of the small room with the twin beds and a window overlooking the driveway. On the wall between the two beds was a poster of a ship. It was an old square rigged wooden ship with all of her sails filled from mainsail to top gallant crashing through white capped seas. She was named UNICORN. In the lower right hand corner was the captain's signature and a large THANK YOU.

'We got this distress signal when the Sara was off of South Carolina," Captain Mark said as he began to open the duffle. "They were taking on water and needed pumps and repairs. Our Captain asked for volunteers who knew wooden boats. Rude Rus and I volunteered. We were lowered from a helicopter because the seas were too rough to approach by boat. It was incredible. What a rush! We were flying around on the end of a cable with a pump trying not to swing into their masts. They finally dropped us on the poop deck. Rude Rus nearly landed on top of me and his pump fell overboard. The ship had a big crack in her hulls below the water line. They must have hit something.

We got my pump running and we patched the hole. They were a training ship and had more students than real crew but Rus and I grew up in Florida and had been patching old wooden boats since we were kids "

"You must have been scared to death up there," the Contessa said.

"Maybe we were," Mark said ,"but we didn't have time to think about it. We just put it on automatic and got the job done. When we finished, we couldn't get back to the Sara so we partied with the crew on the Unicorn until we got to port and they bought us dinner and drinks. It was cool."

Captain Mark brought his duffle bag out on the deck and fished out some bottle rockets. They had a long stem that fit into a bottle with the rocket on top with a short wick. He took out a cigar and a zippo lighter with his ship on the side.

"Not on my deck ," the Contessa warned him about the cigar.

"Yes, Mam," Captain Mark said, " I don't smoke it but when I get it lit I use it to light the fuses. It's easier than with a lighter especially if it's windy. And sometimes the rocket takes off accidentally. It's really a lot of fun."

"Not from the deck," she insisted. "you'll drive the dogs crazy. "

"In between the dunes," Willie said. "Are you coming Waterfall ?"

"It's not because I'm not inter-
ested," Waterfall said. "It's just that I
don't care to join the fun."

She looked at her mother.

"Little boys," the Contessa got
up. "Lets go outside and watch.
Keep the dogs inside."

The boys had no trouble finding
an empty champaigne bottle. Willie
knew the path even in the dark. He
led the way down one dune and up
another to where they found a de-
pression between stands of seaoats
to set up their launching pad. From
their position on top of the dune
they could see the beach in both directions, lit occasionally by the
headlights of a car that turned off at
the ramp. There was no moon and
the sky was full of stars.

The slight breeze off the ocean smelled of salt and sand. There were insect sounds but the breeze kept the mosquitoes off the top of the dune while down in the trough they swarmed.

Captain Mark picked a sandspur out of his foot and finished his can of beer. He lit the cigar while Willie put the first rocket in the bottle.

"Ready for liftoff, " Willie said.

Captain Mark puffed on the cigar until the bright orange glow of the ash lit up their hollow. He touched the hot tip to the fuse and it began to spark. They both stood back.

There was a blast of flame and a loud swoosh and the rocket lifted into the night leaving a trail of

sparks before it exploded a sparkling red shower that was reflected
on the wet sand.

21.

Waterfall and the Contessa sat
with dogs and watched the flame
burst into red fireflies and then they
heard the pop of the explosion. The
dogs began to bark. The white faced
black mutt slinked inside with her
tail down and a look of guilt.

"My God," the Contessa said.
"They set the dunes on fire."

The wind had brought the rocket
back over them and landed in a

patch of dry sea grass. Even in the dark, they could see the shadows moving against the spreading orange line of fire, throwing sand as a wisp of smoke rose and disappeared. There was a pause in the frenzy and they waited. The line of fire was gone, but the smell of smoke drifted up toward them with the sound of two men laughing.

"I don't know what you see in him," the Contessa told Waterfall. "You could do better."

"Maybe somebody like Captain Mark," Waterfall said.

"He has a job," the Contessa said.

"Willie makes me laugh," Waterfall admitted. "I like to laugh."

"How long have you been with him?" the Contessa asked. " He hasn't even bought you a decent set of silver."

"It's not what I see in him," Waterfall said. "It's what he sees in me."

She was beautiful, smart and strong willed like her mother. With Willie it was love at first sight. The first time he saw her, he fell in love with her. And he didn't mind doing what she wanted to do. She was a Florida girl born and bred and when she died she would be Florida dead.

He opened the door at her mother's house. He was with a friend of friend of her brothers who played poker. He was there for the game. They were on their way north to a job in New York. Willie had been forewarned about Waterfall. Her brother said she was crazy. He fell in love with her name. She was one of the beautiful ones. The ones you see in fashion magazines. She was also one of the real ones. The ones you see on the streets.

He rented surfboards from the back of a station wagon while she and her mother ran the shop and factory where the boards were made. He freelanced, scripts and magazine pieces. Some weeks were better than other, but he never quit his day job.

When they got enough money they moved out of her mother's

house. They worked together on video projects and she sold Avon products. Then the Contessa and Waterfall's father acquired some vacant land in the middle of the state that needed development.

They lived in a trailer. It was a single wide mobile home. Waterfall and the Contessa raised calves outside her doublewide. Willie put in wells. He had a pickup truck with a derrick on the back, loads of pipes and hoses. It got him to where he was today.

Waterfall was the real thing. The real Hemingway woman who could work with a man. Walking behind her through a jungle, diving with her underwater, going down a ski trail. When they had their video business, she had charmed Cousteau and the Air Force Thunderbirds. She was comfortable with men but they were not always comfortable with her.

"They got the fire out," the Contessa said. " I hope they don't get caught."

Willie and Captain Mark repositioned the bottle so as to send the rocket out over the beach where the cars ran and there was no vegetation. It was a plan. They could see where a car was coming towards them, its headlights leading the way. It was perfect timing. The rocket didn't explode until it was low enough to light up the red and blue lights that came on in a flash. A search light found Captain Mark standing with a bottle and a rocket in his hands.

"Did you see those kids ?" Captain Mark said as a uniformed officer stood behind his door with one hand on his sidearm and a flashlight in the other shining at his red face and blonde hair. It then caught Willie in the background.

"Ran off that way ," Willie said , pointing to footprints in the sand. "We came down from that house up there to put out a fire."

The two boys came back to the house complaining that the cop had confiscated the rest of the bottle rockets.

Captain Mark had another beer. He sat alone in the dark looking up at the stars and listening to the wind and waves. He would sleep in the "down below", the apartment under the main house.

There were no long goodbyes. Waterfall kissed her mother. She hugged her.

"Pick me up on the way to the doctor tomorrow," Waterfall said in her ear. "Are you sure you'll be all right tonight?"

"Of course. Mark is down below," the Contessa said. "And I have my Mercedes."

"Is Jack coming up here tonight?"

"I don't care if he never comes," the Contessa said. "I think he's forgotten how to get here."

"I love you, " Waterfall said.

When they were in the car. Willie had Waterfall drive. Waterfall slapped her hands. "She gave it to me and then they snatched it away."

They could say that it was be-cause they didn't like Willie but she knew it was because they didn't like her. She didn't fit the proper mold of a housewife. She was a country girl who loved nature from her hideouts in Coconut Grove to the boat and the deep blue sea.

Waterfall was a full time job, but she was worth it. Willie's only complaints were with himself: get-ting older, having lost his boyish charm, the long period of life that it had taken to heal from his surgery, his rage against routine. Other than that he didn't complain. As his mother said, " If you did, what good would it do." He didn't miss his parents because they were with him every day. Their blessing was considered in every decision from life changing choices to cleaning up after himself.

CHAPTER EIGHT

22.

The dogs were all inside slumped in different places in the living room. There was no moonlight so the waves were heard but not seen. Stars were everywhere. The air was clean with a pinch of salt to bring out the flavor.

The Contessa took a deep breath from the upper balcony and caught herself before she coughed. She took a short breath to relax and tears came to her eyes. She closed them and held onto the railing that kept her from falling.

The Contessa knew that she was going to die. Only the pain bothered her. She wanted to put her feet in the ocean again. She wanted to spend another day at the beach.

The day at the beach had ended for Waterfall and Willie. Life like the sea would go on , but the sea would go on longer. They were young with futures longer than their pasts. They would return to the sea; Willie to the boat, Waterfall taking care of her mother at the beach house. Their daughters would grow and babies would have babies. Friends would come and go.

Everyone's face was singed but not burned. A shower and some aloe from a plant in the front yard would take away the sting. When they wet their lips with their tongues it tasted of salt. Whole bodies tingled from the salt water even after a shower. Everyone was tired. They longed for the comfort of cool sheets and a familiar bed.

At the sound of the car in the driveway, the dogs perked up their ears. They sniffed the air and lay back down. Jack came in carrying a briefcase.

He was a large man, over six feet but not overweight. He was handsome middle aged. He wore long pants and a short sleeved white shirt. He took off his heavy brown shoes at the door and wore black socks. He went to the ice box and poured a glass of milk.

The dogs got up but they didn't bark. They growled. A quick "shush" from Jack quieted them. Willie had installed a switch so that the floodlight on the deck could be controlled from inside. It could be a motion detector but then it would confuse the turtles that nested on the beach so it was kept off. Jack turned on the switch.

There was a man outside the sliding glass doors that led to the beach. He was shirtless, barefoot and wore cargo pants that hung down lower on one side because there was something heavy in his pocket. The dogs crowded around Jack as he went to the door. The man didn't back away obviously not scared of the dogs. He had disheveled red hair, unshaven for days and a permanent sun burn. His eyes were glazed and sensitive to the light.

When Jack was a young man, he read How To Win Friends and Influence People. It was empathy that he told Waterfall was the most important attitude in life. There was good in everyone.

23.

Waterfall had interviewed her father and recorded his story for Veteran's Day. She remembered growing up hearing him screaming and falling out of bed at night. He had never talked about the war.

"I went ashore on D Day," he never blinked. "They never show you all the bodies we had to wade through to get to the beach. I was a forward observer directing fire at the enemy. I was a pilot in the Army. I was flying a reconnaisance plane. It was a small plane and they could shoot at me but I couldn't shoot back. They told me that after I had flown twenty-two missions I would be rotated out. All of the other pilots were dead, so they told me I had to fly twenty-two more missions. Every time I completed them, they told me that after a few more flights..."

He paused and took a deep breath.

"On my eighty-second mission I spotted German troops in their green uniforms at a bridge head and I called in the coordinants for our artillery. They hit the target. When I returned to the base they told me that the Canadians wore green uniforms also. There were many casualties. After that I couldn't go up again. I told them that I wouldn't fly."

The Contessa was sitting next to him while he spoke. She held his hand.

"They put me in handcuffs and took me away. I thought they were going to send me back to the states to be court-marstialed. On the ship, the doctors examined me. When I told them my experience they put me in a hospital where I met this very attractive ambulance driver."

The Contessa looked at him and smiled. He looked back at her and his eyes moistened. She squeezed his hand.

"Then they gave me a medal," he said.

24.

"Can I help you," Jack said through the screen.

"I'm hungry, " the man said. "Do you have any money?"

"Let me fix you a sandwich," Jack said and went back to the kitchen where he quickly found two slices of bread and some salami from the refrigerator . He opened the screen and handed it to the man who took it but did not eat. The dogs paid attention but did not get up.

"Do you have any money ?" the man said.

Jack reached into his pants pocket and took out some small bills and handed them to the man.

"Anything to drink ?" the man asked.

"Only water, " Jack said. "But there's a convenience store just two blocks from here. You can buy something there."

The man stuck the bills into his heavy pants pocket and paused for a second. Then he changed his mind and went down to the drive-way and onto the highway. He had no trouble finding the store. It was late and there was no traffic. He went inside and asked the night clerk for some cigarettes and a beer. Then he pulled a gun on the young man and had him empty the register. He left with his score and was walking along the road a short distance away when the police pulled him over and arrested him without incident.

25.

Jack went upstairs to the Contessa's bedroom. She had known he was there from the first sound of his car in the driveway. It wasn't a Mercedes. When he came into the room to undress and then went to clean up in the bathroom, she pretended to be asleep with her back to him. He rolled into bed next to her. She moved next to him and fell asleep.

A day at the beach had ended.

It was a good day.

THE END

www.ingramcontent.com/pod-product-compliance
Lightning Source LLC
Chambersburg PA
CBHW070930180626
46817CB00003B/1223